Baby's First
JAILBREAK

Written by
Jim Whalley

Illustrated by
Stephen Collins

BLOOMSBURY

BLOOMSBURY CHILDREN'S BOOKS
Bloomsbury Publishing Plc
50 Bedford Square, London, WC1B 3DP, UK

BLOOMSBURY, BLOOMSBURY CHILDREN'S BOOKS and the Diana logo are trademarks of Bloomsbury Publishing Plc
First published in Great Britain by Bloomsbury Publishing Plc

ISBN 978 1 4088 9183 4 (HB)
ISBN 978 1 4088 9181 0 (PB)
ISBN 978 1 4088 9182 7 (eBook)

1 3 5 7 9 10 8 6 4 2

Printed and bound in China by Leo Paper Products, Heshan, Guangdong
All papers used by Bloomsbury Publishing Plc are natural,
recyclable products from wood grown in well managed forests.
The manufacturing processes conform to the environmental
regulations of the country of origin.

To find out more about our authors and books
visit www.bloomsbury.com and sign up for our newsletters

JW: For Mum and Dad,
thanks for everything.
SC: For little Isaac
and Baby Stella.

Perhaps you heard the story
of a baby boy named Frank,
who turned his home into a zoo
by stealing from a bank.

The problem was he got caught out
and so, to pay his debts,
Frank's mum and dad charged visitors
to see his many pets.

TO THE SHARKS

FEEDING TIMES

Rainforest Sounds

Soon Baby Frank was famous
and each day there was a queue –
the whole town couldn't wait to
see the baby with a zoo.

But, over time, Frank's parents saw
their crowds were getting small,
until the day that Dad announced,
"There's no one here at all!"

Out on a walk one afternoon,
the reason became clear –
a vain and pampered baby
had just stolen their idea.

The other baby's name was Bruce –
his mum and dad were rich.
They'd had his zoo constructed
on their private polo pitch.

They had tigers wearing tutus and a dancing chimpanzee.

There were penguins dressed as waiters handing ice creams out for free.

It was during a performance
by some acrobatic deer
that Mum declared, "I've had enough.
Let's get out of here."

As they went out through the gift shop,
Dad sighed, "They've got us beat.
Our animals don't dance at all.
How can we compete?"

That night Frank had a visitor – a penguin escapee
who, using squawks and flaps and mime, conveyed a heartfelt plea.
"Please save us from that baby Bruce. All he does is train us.
I don't think he likes penguins much – he just wants to be famous."

"Each morning we get up at dawn
to practise dance routines,
and sometimes we don't break for lunch –
he treats us like machines!"

Frank agreed to help and got his crayons out to make
a clever plan so he could lead a daring prison break.

By two a.m. the plan was set and Frank was on his way.
He took along some friends of his to help him save the day.

Problem One was getting in, as Bruce had built a wall,
but Frank was ready with a friend whose neck was very tall.

The penguins' door was bolted shut
but opened with a creak
once the lock was neatly picked
by hummingbird's long beak.

Then in swung orangutan and grabbed the penguin huddle...

And, as they passed the tortoise house, a cry came from a shell...

to carry them to freedom in a long-armed, hairy cuddle.

The tortoises weren't happy, so Frank took them all as well.

He set free the hyena
and the wombats and the ape...

...till every creature in the zoo had joined the great escape.

Next morning Frank was woken by his parents looking troubled. They asked him, "Can you tell us why our animals have doubled?"

Frank pointed to the penguins
sleeping soundly on the floor,
but before he could explain,
they heard a knock upon their door.

Bruce had brought his mum and she was looking very cross.
She said, "My son thinks you're behind our recent creature loss."

They stormed into the house but, as they looked around the place,
Bruce's mum soon lightened up – a smile spread on her face.

"Brucie, darling, can't you see, these animals are cheerful.
They simply can't belong to us – all of ours are tearful."

And so they both departed,
as Bruce let out a yell.
Mum said, "Forget the animals –
they made an awful smell."

After that, it wasn't long
before Frank's crowds returned,
and soon the bank had been repaid
with all the cash he earned.

Everyone agreed the zoo was better than before...

...especially once space was found –
by purchasing next door.

And, as for Bruce, his quest for fame should take off very soon...

He's working on a rocket ship
to take him to the moon!